CHOPSTICKS FROM
AMERICA

By Elaine Hosozawa-Nagano ❖ Illustrated by Masayuki Miyata

LIBRARY OF CONGRESS CATALOGING - IN- PUBLICATION DATA

Hosozawa-Nagano, Elaine, 1953-
Chopsticks From America / Written by
Elaine Hosozawa-Nagano : illustrated by Masayuki
Miyata —1st ed.
        p.   cm.

Summary:
When their family moves to Japan, two Japanese
American children find that they need to make a
lot of adjustments.

ISBN No. 1-879965-11-9 : $16.95
1. Japanese Americans — Fiction.
2. Japan— Fiction.
I. Miyata, Masayuki, ill.
II. Title

PZ7.H795Ch   1994
[E]—dc20

        93-45795
        CIP
        AC

This is a New Book, Written and Illustrated
Especially for Polychrome Books
First Edition, June, 1995

Designed, produced and published by
Polychrome Publishing Corporation
4509 North Francisco Avenue,
Chicago, Illinois 60625-3808
(312) 478-4455 Fax: (312) 478-0786

Editorial Director, Sandra S. Yamate
Art Director/Designer, Heather Mark Chen
Production Coordinator, Brian M. Witkowski

Printed in Hong Kong
10 9 8 7 6 5 4 3 2 1

ISBN 1-879965-11-9

THIS BOOK BELONGS TO

DEDICATION

To my dear daughter, Tiffany, who is relentless
in her requests for "another story."

TABLE OF CONTENTS

MADE IN THE USA

Kevin and I are concerned. We've been told that our family will be moving to Japan to live there for a few years. I'm not sure what to expect. I just know that it'll be different.

I am Tiffany and I am eleven years old. I have shiny black hair, fair skin, and my mother has always told me to be proud of my eyes because they give me that special "Asian look." I am Japanese American. My younger brother Kevin is only five. To look at my younger brother and me, you can tell that we are related. The resemblance is strong. Together with our Mom and Dad, we live a happy life on Sycamore Drive. But all this is about to change.

What lies ahead for both of us is yet to be discovered. It seems that Dad is being sent on an assignment for his company, and that means that the whole family will be moving to Japan. Japan! That sounds so far away to me. We have never been to Japan. I'm worried.

What should we expect? Both Kevin and I were born and raised in the United States. Oh sure, we're aware of some Japanese customs; Mom and Dad made sure of that. We observe the traditional Girls' Day and Boys' Day celebrations; we participate in the annual church "O-bon Festival;" we are raised as Buddhists; and every New Year we help with "Mochi-tsuki." But in our everyday life we eat hamburgers, french fries, pizza, spaghetti, barbecue steaks, tacos and the usual stuff. Occasionally, we eat using "O-hashi" or chopsticks and have a Japanese dinner with miso soup which Mom prepares. Kevin and I both go to Japanese language school because Mom and Dad feel that it is important to be bilingual. They say being bilingual will serve us well one day. But do you suppose this has prepared us for living in Japan!? I don't think so.

With these thoughts running through my mind, I turned and looked at Kevin. He was busy playing with his Lego building set. He was building something very tall and very blue. It didn't seem like he understood that moving would have an effect on us, or maybe he didn't care.

I'd say I'm pretty experienced about "new" things; after all, I'm eleven. As for Kevin, he's a mere child and more timid than me. This means that as Kevin's O-nechan or big sister, I'll just have to look out for him. Being older, it's only natural that I'm the more worldly one.

Doubting that Kevin was really aware of what was about to happen to him, I asked, "Kevin, are you excited about going to Japan?"

"NO!" he answered, practically shouting.

Well, if it wasn't clear to me before, it was clear to me now. Kevin knew what was about to happen and he didn't like the idea any more than I did.

Mom and Dad seemed concerned about Kevin's reaction to the big news. Seeing the concern on their faces, I didn't admit that, just like my little brother, I didn't like the idea. I wasn't happy. No more American television! No more videotapes and movies! No more hamburgers and french fries from McDonald's! It was unthinkable! Still, as far as I could tell, we were going, so I decided to set a good example for Kevin and not make matters worse by complaining.

Over the next couple of weeks we packed up the whole house. We sold some things, gave other things away, and some things we would just have to leave in storage. "We can't take everything," Dad kept saying. Mom would look at him sadly, knowing he was right but not knowing how she could possibly sell or pack away and leave behind almost all that was familiar to us. After all, we had a household of things that we had been accumulating for over eleven years.

I packed away my dolls, all their clothes, furniture and cars. I packed my stuffed animals and games, kitchen set-up and dishes, and many of my books. Dad says I have "tons" of books, but I feel I don't have enough. I've read each of them more than a few times. I had to pack and store all these things. I knew they would be too heavy to pack and take with us. As I thought more about the move, I could feel myself getting angry. Why did Dad have to get an assignment in Japan now? I didn't want to leave my friends and my school. And what about my dance lessons? I continued to pack.

Kevin went through his possessions and announced that he just had to take everything he owned with him: trucks, cars, trains, toy soldiers, boats, his Lego building set, but most importantly, his favorite friend, "Freckles." Freckles was a spotted, stuffed dog that Kevin got as a present when he was born. Freckles looked worn out; he was pretty shabby and soiled and was even tearing in spots.

"You don't want to take that old thing. You can get a newer, cuter stuffed animal in Japan," I told him.

"No. Freckles is mine, and I'm not leaving without him," Kevin stated firmly.

This was going to be tougher than I thought. Not only was I not happy about this move, my brother obviously was going to resist new surroundings any way that he could, even if that meant not parting with anything he owned--and that, it seemed, was just what he had decided to do. Kevin can be very stubborn at times.

I could just see it now: we will be walking the streets of Tokyo and Kevin will be trailing behind, clinging to old Freckles and complaining the whole time, "I'm hungry, I'm thirsty, can we stop now?" I thought about it for awhile and decided that it would be best for all of us if I tried to comfort Kevin. If he felt better about this move, he might even begin to get excited. Maybe I would, too.

"Kev," I said, "just think about it. We'll be able to see where Jichan and Bachan (Grandpa and Grandma) were raised. I remember Jichan saying that it is very green and beautiful in Japan." Then I recalled that Kevin really enjoyed his last fishing trip and so I said, "Kev, I bet there are lots of lakes and streams where you can fish! Oh, Kevin! Won't that be great? You love to fish!" I exclaimed. I was beginning to feel some imagined excitement myself as I tried to convince Kevin that this move might turn out to be wonderful after all.

Kevin wasn't about to allow himself to get excited. He was not happy about the move and nothing I could say would make him feel better.

IS THIS JAPAN?

O nce we boarded the plane there would be no turning back. Kevin seemed to understand this, too. He sat beside me on the plane, clinging to Freckles as if to comfort the stuffed dog. I had secretly hoped that Dad's assignment would be changed, or that Mom would protest enough to make Dad change his mind, or that something would happen which would cause our parents to give the whole thing a second thought. But no such luck. We were going, and we wouldn't turn back now.

We landed outside Tokyo, which at first looked like any American city to me. It is very modern and has tall buildings, fancy department stores and a lot of activity along its streets. Tokyo is a very busy place, even busier than Los Angeles or New York, but there was a difference. Everywhere you looked there were people and most of them were Japanese. They were rushing here and there. They rush because they have to be somewhere. They rush because they're late getting somewhere. They rush because they have to get back to somewhere.

I'll admit, I was a little excited by all the activity that surrounded me, but I think Kevin was secretly glad to know that we wouldn't be living in Tokyo. We would be living in Saitama Prefecture, somewhere outside of Tokyo. We would stay in Tokyo, however, for a few days. To Kevin, Tokyo was too crowded. I took his hand.

As we walked, I saw that the signs we passed were written mainly in

Japanese. Then, I spotted a McDonald's out of the corner of my eye; at least Japan had McDonald's. Still, I felt a pang of homesickness. We looked like the people we passed but we were still different. We didn't talk like them. We didn't dress like them, I thought. While holding onto Kevin's hand and walking, I felt like we were a pair of chopsticks among other chopsticks, only we were from America.

Just as I had predicted, Kevin began his wailing as we toured the Tokyo streets. "I'm hungry, I'm thirsty. Can we stop here?" Kevin was at it.

Mom and Dad finally got so tired of hearing this from Kevin that they relented. We stopped at a small udon shop for lunch; that's a noodle shop. The old woman who served us spoke to us in Japanese. Mom ordered and we were soon served bowls of noodles in hot soy broth with green onions and vegetables. My udon was steaming wildly. It was very hot and tasted wonderfully familiar and delicious! Yum! We were so hungry that we ate quietly, even Kevin.

Something started to happen to me while I ate my lunch. I felt myself warming up to Japan, not only because my noodles were hot but because I was comforted somehow. Eating that simple bowl of noodles that I had often eaten in the United States, I realized that not everything in Japan would seem foreign and strange. In fact, this familiar bowl of udon seemed even tastier in Japan.

The old woman must have known we were "gaijin" or "foreigners" because she asked Mom where we were from. After a little discussion with the woman, Mom explained to us what the lady had told her. Noodles are eaten all year round in Japan, but in hot weather a favorite is soba, made from buckwheat flour and served with wasabi which is a green horseradish. Somen, white wheat noodles that are very thin, is also a favorite during hot months because it is served cold, or "five flavors" gomoku style, with egg, chicken, fish or various vegetables. Of course we had known that; we've had soba and somen back in the United States. In our hurry to sit down and eat, however, we had forgotten about these dishes and had ordered based upon the sign outside that read "Udon." The menu, after all, was written only in Japanese!

I looked over at Kevin. He had finished his bowl of noodles, drank his water, and seemed thoroughly content. For that matter, Freckles seemed content, too. Dad announced that we were ready to move on with our walking tour. He acknowledged the satisfying meal to the nice lady, saying, "Oishi-katta," or "it was delicious," and we were on our way.

Since we were only planning to stay in Tokyo for a few days, Mom and Dad tried to schedule as many things for us to see as they could. One of our first stops was to the department stores.

The department stores are really very nice. "Everything looks shiny, new and clean, including the floors," commented Kevin. On the lower levels of the department stores foods of all kinds are sold from various counters: snack item, hot foods to take home for dinner, "musubi" or rice balls, sushi with lots and lots of different toppings on them, cakes, candies, desserts, rice crackers, drinks, fruits, and anything you might want if you were grocery shopping.

"Mom," wailed Kevin, "we could have eaten here."

Although we were quite full from lunch, we tried various things. Dad was interested in tasting dried fish, meat items such as ginger fried pork and beef, and different kinds of musubi and sushi. Mom wanted to taste the pretty dessert items and the many pickled vegetable tsukemono which were sold in a rainbow variety of colors and textures, from crunchy to squishy. I was intrigued by the different ice creams and yogurt flavors, and Kevin, who is forever asking for yet "another drink," was in awe of the many different flavored beverages that were available. "Tiffany, I bet I could have a different drink for every meal, every day of the month," he exclaimed excitedly. Of course he was exaggerating. Before we left, we purchased box lunches or "bento" to eat later in our hotel room.

Although it was late June, it rained. A couple of days it rained very heavily. On those days you could see umbrellas everywhere. From our hotel window, they looked like blossoms floating through the streets of the city. The amazing thing to me is that people would leave their umbrellas right outside of stores, restaurants, and even hotels. I remembered how often Mom had reminded me back in the States not to leave my umbrella or any belongings unattended. "Someone will just take it," she would warn. I thought it strange that these people didn't seem to worry about that.

During the following days, we saw a traditional tea ceremony; flower arranging called ikebana; and heard a woman play a musical string instrument called the koto. We even saw a puppet show known as Bunraku, where the puppets used are the largest I've ever seen. It was almost like seeing a live stage performance. All this was exciting to me. I had seen some of these things before in the United States, but seeing them demonstrated in Japan made them interesting and more exciting. Kevin thought they were boring.

A few days later, we rode the train to our new home. This was a thrill for Kevin and me. We had never ridden a train before, that is, not a real one. I began to wonder about our new home. From what I could see of the scenery we were passing, we weren't going to live in a big city; we were going to live in the COUNTRY. I looked over at Kevin; he seemed calmer now that we were out of the hectic city. He looked so cute sitting in his seat hugging Freckles. He really seemed to be enjoying this train ride.

Even though I had thought it was ridiculous that Kevin had to carry Freckles on the plane and through all of Tokyo, I realized at this moment that Freckles had been a great help to Kevin during our travel. Freckles was a pal like no other to Kevin, a pal who had seen and shared a lot of good and bad times with him. Of course, Freckles looked as though he had been through a lot, too. He certainly was old and tattered, but obviously he was still very special to Kevin.

I knew my funny little brother could seem strange, and even weird, at times, but just then I really understood how he felt. In the beginning, I wasn't thrilled about this trip either. I wanted Kevin to know that I understood how he felt, so I leaned over and gave him a big hug. He looked up at me appreciatively. It was one of those rare moments between brother and sister when you know you are "brother and sister" after all.

Kevin and I must have fallen asleep, because the next thing I knew, Mom and Dad were waking us and hurrying to gather up our things. Our stop was coming up and we would need to get off the train quickly. Then I heard the announcement as the train paused briefly in the station before it would zip off toward its next stop. We had to get off now. "Kevin, come quick! Follow me," I said as I hurried after Mom. Dad trailed behind making certain we all got off.

We made it! We had our bags in hand and Dad was leading the way. Off we went in search of a taxi to take us to our new home.

Suddenly, Kevin let out a cry. "Freckles! Freckles! Mom! Where's Freckles?"

Everybody looked around but Freckles was not in sight. We must have left Freckles on the train! In all the excitement to get off the train, we had left Freckles behind! Kevin looked panic stricken, then horrified, and then too unhappy to even describe.

I thought quickly. "Lost and Found!" I shrieked. "There must be a Lost and Found, Dad."

Dad swiftly asked one of the station attendants where the Lost and Found Office was located and he hurried to it while Mom, Kevin and I sat and waited on a nearby bench with our luggage.

Twenty minutes or so later Dad returned. "It's still too early for someone to have turned it in, but the Transportation Office called the train and spoke with the Conductor. They've had the car we were seated in checked. Seems it's not there. We'll just have to wait and see. I left our telephone number where we can be reached," said Dad.

Did he say it was too early for someone to turn IT in? Freckles had now been reduced to an "IT!"

I detected a tear on Kevin's cheek and suddenly my heart sank and I felt sad, too. We tried to comfort him but Kevin could not be comforted. There wasn't more anyone could do. Poor Kevin.

LOOKING FOR ANOTHER FRECKLES

We arrived at our new home, all of us but Freckles, of course. It's a quiet little community, with small houses that line up on both sides of irregular streets that wind through town. Green hills surround the small town and beyond the tiny houses are wide open meadows and tea fields.

That first day Kevin waited by the telephone in case we got a call about Freckles. Dad phoned the train station later that night but still Freckles had not been turned in at the Lost and Found. Two more days passed as we checked each day for Freckles. No luck. I just knew that we would never see Freckles again and I think Kevin knew it too.

The days passed and Kevin and I were still trying to get accustomed to Saitama. The Japanese school year begins in June, so we went to school each day. Few of the other students spoke English. When I tried to speak in Japanese, they would giggle; even the teachers would smile at my accent. Going to school was lonely. I was glad Kevin was around at home.

As we played and ran around outside our new home in T-shirts and shorts, neighbors often asked us from where we had come. "A-me-ri-ka?" they would ask. It surprised me how often America was the first guess. I wondered if it was the way we played or perhaps the way we talked. I guessed that it might also be by the clothes we wore; after all, they hadn't always heard us speak before they asked if we were from "A-me-ri-ka." Mom had brought along a few old yukata sets for Kevin and me that she had found in our

Grandmother's trunk in the United States. Kevin and I decided to wear them. Hardly anyone wore kimonos or yukatas anymore, but we preferred them because they were surprisingly comfortable to wear. Besides that, they were our meager attempt to fit in and be Japanese.

After that first week without Freckles, Dad took me aside and asked if I thought it would be a good idea to buy a real dog. A dog would keep us company. A dog would be a playmate. A dog would take the place of Freckles, I suspected. I thought it would be good for Kevin. I knew Kevin missed Freckles terribly. A real dog would be great fun for Kevin--and for me, too.

When Dad took us to the pet store to look for a dog, Kevin and I didn't really know what kind of dog we wanted. Dad thought perhaps a small dog, like a Chihuahua, would be easy to care for and would make a good pet. Kevin liked it. I thought it was too small.

"We need a bigger dog," I said. "That Chihuahua is so small, I'm afraid we might accidentally step on it."

"Well, Tiffany," argued Kevin, "he won't take up any room. Look, he even fits inside of a shoe. If you're afraid you might step on him, just look where you walk!" he snapped. I got the feeling that he wanted to take the first dog that was offered to him.

"The St. Bernard is a pretty big dog," I pointed out.
"I think he's a little too big, don't you, Kev?" asked Dad.
"Uh huh," agreed Kevin.

"How about a Basset Hound?" asked Dad.
The Basset looked like a very slow moving dog.
It had droopy eyes and ears and he looked very sad.
He seemed to me to really need a home, but Kevin didn't agree.
"Not our home," Kevin stated firmly. My little brother
could be such a pain sometimes.

"A Bull Dog would make a terrific guard dog," said Dad,
moving on to the other dogs that were available. It was true. The Bull
Dog looked pretty tough. Kevin and I didn't necessarily want a guard dog.
We wanted a smart but playful dog. He just didn't seem right for us. He
didn't seem like the kind of dog that would be very playful.

"Yes, I think he would make a fine watch dog," Dad tried again.
A watch dog! Was that all Dad could think about? What about a dog that
would be a playmate, a companion, a pal? The more Dad tried to convince
us that the Bull Dog would be a good choice, the more certain Kevin and I
became that he was not the right dog for us.

~~~~~~~~~~

When it became clear that we wouldn't be convinced
about the merits of owning a Bull Dog, Dad said, "Poodles are nice."
They were fluffy and cute and all but they also seemed too noisy.
They seemed to need too much attention. They really weren't very
playful, just needy. Besides that, Kevin and I couldn't agree on
which color poodle we liked best.

~~~~~~~~~~

This Pekingese sure has a cute pug face," said Dad.

Neither Kevin nor I thought it was very cute.

~~~~~~~~~~

Then I happened upon a Russian Hound. He was a handsome looking dog, black and white, kind of large with a pointy snout and long legs. I liked him immediately. As I turned to Kevin to point the dog out to him, Kevin seemed engaged in conversation with a Dachshund.

"I found a dog!" he exclaimed. "Tif, I found a dog I like!" The Dachshund was a smaller, friendly dog with a long body and a shiny, beautiful black and brown coat. I wondered why Kevin liked such small dogs. Maybe it was because he was still pretty small himself.

What to do now? I had found a dog I liked. Kevin had found one, too. Too bad it wasn't the same dog.

"Only one dog," reminded Dad, "just one."

Well, there we were. How could we decide?

Dad was visibly frustrated by this time. "I guess we'll just have to pass on a dog until another time," he announced. With that, home we went . . . without a dog.

CAN THIS BE HOME FOR A WHILE?

Kevin seems to have taken a liking to his new surroundings. He loves the scenic outdoors and claims that the greenery of Japan is a different shade of green than in the United States. It's a brighter, more lively green, he says. Because of this, I suppose, he is always outdoors. Under our parents' watchful eyes, he takes walks, plays in the fields, explores, and even draws while outdoors. He's always liked to draw. He would draw for long periods of time at home in the United States. He'd take a pencil or marker and draw what he described as planes, cars, cartoon characters or super heroes. I didn't think it was possible, but Kevin seems to enjoy drawing even more since coming to Japan, and as time passes, I can see that he is getting very good at it.

There are lots of rivers near our place, and Kevin just loves this about our new home, too. Not only does he include rivers in many of his drawings, but he seems to like to spend his time near the water. He studies the fish that live in them and he will sit by a river for hours sometimes, just watching.

About the only thing to do around our new home is fish and that suits Kevin just fine. He has been very determined to catch a "big fish" ever since we first arrived. It didn't matter what kind of fish, so long as it was big.

I never liked fishing much, but Kevin insisted that I give it a try, so one day, I did.

That day, I nearly caught what I'm positive must have been one of Kevin's "big fish." Why, it could have even been two or three fish all connected together because it put up a good fight. I tugged and tugged on my fishing rod and pulled and pulled but in the end it got away. I really don't understand why people make such a big deal of fishing. Kevin loves it. He fishes as often as he can, almost two or three times a week. If he discovers nothing else, the fishing in Japan alone will make Kevin's trip a memorable one.

As the days go by, Kevin seems happier and happier. I, however, become more and more depressed. What seemed like the beginning of an exciting adventure in Tokyo, now seems like a bore. We live in the country. The children who live near us speak very little English and our Japanese, in spite of lessons, isn't that good. Few of the children at our school speak English and none live nearby. There isn't much to do here but try to enjoy NATURE, which is easy to do if you like that sort of thing. I don't.

There is one nice thing about our place, though, and that is the many tea fields that are in and around our town. There are mounds and mounds of tea bushes growing in neat little rows that you can see from our house, no matter which direction you look.

Even though the season for it is almost over, I learned that some people in our town were still growing and cultivating tea leaves. Thinking that it could be fun to pick tea leaves, I convinced Kevin to try something that I wanted to do.

Okay, I'll admit it was hard work. But it was kind of fun, too, or at least I

tell everyone it was. Kevin thought it was tiring and boring and he didn't hesitate to say so. He soon began to whine, as he always does when he doesn't want to do something. "I'm tired. I'm thirsty. Let's get something to drink Tiffany, pl-e-e-ease. I don't care about tea leaf picking," he wailed. Kevin could be so trying at times.

DIFFICULT TIMES

As Fall began to approach, the leaves on the trees turned bright red and orange. I had never seen such colorful trees before. "Kevin, what do you think about these trees?" I asked. "Aren't they pretty? Kevin, we've been in Japan for several months now. Do you like Japan? I'm not sure I do. I guess we should make the best of it, shouldn't we? Kevin, what do you think? Kevin?"

"Tiffany, I can't get my ball down from the tree." Kevin didn't seem to hear me. Sometimes he drifts into his own little world, unaware of his surroundings. I wondered if Kevin ever thought about whether this visit to Japan was a good thing. He didn't seem unhappy at all these days. I'm not sure I'll ever get used to my new surroundings. To me, it seems that we've been away from our home, school, and friends for too long a time. Unlike Kevin, I'm always wondering if this trip was a good thing.

I found it a little strange, even peculiar, that Kevin is no longer fussing about this move. He can be difficult when he wants to be.

For instance, Kevin never liked persimmons before, but he says this fruit tastes better to him in Japan. How can that be? We never saw persimmons growing in the United States, but in Japan they are plentiful. They are orange in color and grow on trees like oranges, but they taste nothing like oranges. There are two types of persimmons that I know of: the hard sweet type and the soft bitter type. Kevin now likes them both! Since he developed a taste for them, he wants to pick them all the time. He'll pick them right off the tree and eat them. An old persimmon tree behind our house was very tall and its persimmons seemed to loom menacingly at Kevin. Picking persimmons, therefore, became a challenge to him. The harder it was for him to pick a persimmon off the tree, the tastier he claimed it was once he took a bite out of it. Picking persimmons became another favorite pastime of Kevin's. I helped, but didn't find picking them enjoyable at all. I've noticed that the simplest of things seem to give Kevin joy these days.

It poured for days during the end of September. Kevin and I weren't used to this kind of weather, and even a simple little trip to the local store caused me major grief. On our way, I broke the strap to one of my geta, the wooden thongs I liked to wear. I wondered why everything in Japan had to be so difficult! I felt stressed!

The truth is I missed my home back in the U.S. I missed American movies, my friends, and American television! Trying to understand Japanese television was a lot of work, and it took the fun out of watching. By the time I could figure out half of what was being said, the screen would flash to a new scene to be translated too. It gave me a headache. How I wished I had paid more attention in Japanese school.

When Dad came home from work, I told him about our day. I complained to him that there wasn't anything to do around here. I complained that everything in Japan seemed so difficult. The rain and even

my geta gave me trouble today. Why does it have to be this way?

Dad looked at me and said "Tiffany, the way you look at a thing will affect your experience with it."

Well what did that mean? How cryptic could he get? The way I looked at a thing would cause me to experience it the way I see it? Is that what he meant? Or did he mean that the way I looked at a thing would affect the way I experienced it? Or were these the same thing? I felt pretty frustrated at this point, and decided not to think about it any more.

Thanksgiving and Christmas came and went. Our family celebrated "just as we always had in the United States," said Dad. He was mainly correct, except for a few pretty big "minor" changes. Take the turkey for example; we had roasted chicken instead. And instead of dinner rolls, we had rice. We had the usual array of vegetables, for which I never cared much, but instead of cranberry sauce, we had tsukemono or pickled cucumbers and turnips.

Christmas was better, I thought. There was never any set dinner fare or menu for Christmas. Mom just prepared whatever she thought would be nice. Each year it was a different meal. So Christmas dinner, which consisted of ham, sashimi or raw fish, and numerous colorful vegetable dishes, was fine with me. We exchanged presents and even had a Christmas tree decorated with new ornaments, some which were purchased and others which we'd

made ourselves. But I couldn't get used to hearing familiar traditional carols sung in Japanese, which we heard on television and in the stores as we did our Christmas shopping. This was another painful reminder to me that we were in Japan during my favorite holiday season, Christmas. The holidays certainly didn't seem the same to me. "They're just different Tiffany," Kevin said, "the holidays aren't bad, they're just different."

"I can accept that," I said. Secretly I thought, I guess I had better try. "Well, it doesn't matter, Kevin," I continued, "soon the New Year will be here and we'll have mochi-tsuki to do, just like at home. I can't wait." I whispered under my breath, "And it can't get here soon enough."

Something was definitely happening to us. I'll admit that neither one of us liked the idea of coming to Japan in the first place. But wasn't I the one who was more excited once we got here? Now it seemed that Kevin enjoyed Japan more than I did. I thought that Kevin would need help adjusting, but it turned out that Kevin was doing just fine, even without Freckles. In fact, Kevin had discovered his own adventures in our new surroundings. Even a down pouring of rain wouldn't dampen his feelings. What was it Dad had said the other day? "How you look at something affects the way you see it." Somehow, I thought his words applied here, but I wasn't quite sure how. What exactly had he meant?

NEW BEGINNINGS

Mochi-tsuki is observed before the New Year. It's a time when Kevin and I would help Mom and Dad make mochi which would be eaten during O-shogatsu or the New Year holiday. Mochi is a sticky cake made of sweet rice and it is one of Kevin's favorite foods.

This year we would "pound" the mochi with wooden mallets, Dad declared. We had seen this tradition done before, but now it's common to use an electric machine to mix the mochi. Why bother pounding it, I wondered. Mom brought out the hot tub of steamy sweet rice and poured it into a tree stump that had been partially hollowed into the shape of a bowl. Dad let Kevin try the wooden mallet. Mom said I could try to turn the mochi between the pounding. We began.

The mallet was so heavy that when Kevin swung it over his head, he nearly toppled over. The rice was so hot that I had difficulty touching it, much less turning it. We laughed at the commotion and the comical sight of each other. Then, before the mochi could get cold, Dad and Mom took over.

"Making mochi is a lot harder work than eating mochi," commented Kevin as we helped shape the pounded mochi into individual pieces.

We all laughed at the silly but simple truth he spoke.

"Much of life is like that," said Dad. "There's a lot of work and preparation that goes into the wonderful foods we enjoy. There's a lot of preparation in everyday life, whether it is work, play, material things or activities we enjoy.

We must appreciate all aspects of what we see, do, and eat."

This was all very Buddhist sounding to me, but it made sense.

Kevin, looking red and tired, began his whining. "I'm hot, I'm tired, I'm thirsty."

"Okay, Kev, let's take a break and get something to drink," I said. I knew that I could use the break, too.

I guess you could say our mochi-tsuki was a success. As we worked, neighbors soon came out and joined us. They brought their cooked mochi-gome and we all helped each other by pounding what seemed like tons and tons of sweet rice. At the end, all the families who participated took home plenty of the white, sticky, sweet rice cakes. It may be superstitious of us, but with such a plentiful yield of mochi, we all felt assured that the New Year would be a prosperous one.

As the excitement of the New Year settled down, we continued our daily routine. Even though the weather was cold and snowy, Kevin still seemed to enjoy being outdoors. As for me, it was all I could do to keep from freezing. Life still seemed a bit of a bore. The only thing I had to look forward to was Girls' Day.

In Japan, March 3rd is celebrated as Girls' Day. Girls dress in their prettiest kimonos and people display beautiful decorative dolls of the Emperor and Empress and the Royal Court. Branches of cherry blossom flowers and sweet rice cakes in pastel colors are also displayed.

In America, Mom would always bring out my decorative dolls to display, which made me feel kind of special. On this particular day of this year, however, I am feeling especially grumpy; we have been in Japan for almost nine months and I still don't feel quite at home.

Kevin never paid much attention to Girls' Day in the past. He always ran outdoors to play since this day had nothing to do with boys. This year, however, he sensed my unhappiness and said, "Tiffany, I'm gonna spend the whole day with you. We can play anything you want."

And he did. He stayed with me all day just as he had promised. By the end of the day I almost wished he hadn't promised that; he was beginning to bother me.

I guess I just haven't adjusted to my new surroundings as well as I thought I would. Kevin seems to be doing just fine though; he hardly ever seems unhappy. In fact, I think he's actually enjoying himself quite a bit. The truth is, I find it hard to believe. Funny little Kevin, my whiny little brother whom I thought would have such a difficult time adjusting, was doing better than me!

My glum mood persisted silently until Boys' Day. On May 5th, all of Japan celebrates Boys' Day and wherever you look you see "Koinobori," fish kites flown on poles. The fish tails, which are long and flowing, flap in the wind. It really is a pretty sight.

Kevin seemed especially proud on this day, rather like a pumped up

rooster when it walks around the chicken coop. He wore a samurai hat that he had made out of an old newspaper and went around all day acting very bossy. I suppose that it was his day to celebrate so I good naturedly put up with it. After all, I remembered how generously Kevin gave of his time to me on Girls' Day.

Kevin knows his big sister very well. Even though he had learned to enjoy his situation by keeping a good attitude about it, and by seeing the good in all that surrounded him, he knew that I was still having a hard time settling in.

Shortly afterwards, Dad walked in and said, "Our neighbor Mr. Matsushita, says this dog followed him home two days ago and won't leave. He seems to be a stray. Mr. Matsushita wants to know if you want this dog Kevin, since it's Boys' Day and all. What do you kids think?" We looked up and saw a dog. We weren't quite sure what kind of dog it was. It just looked like an ordinary dog. He was kind of medium sized, kind of spotted, kind of friendly, and lonely looking as if in need of a good home. He was, well, ordinary. But I liked him immediately.

Kevin looked at him, and then at me. "Do you like him Tiffany?" Kevin asked. " Well, yes, I like him," I said. I knew Kevin preferred smaller dogs, and I secretly waited for him to give some reason why we shouldn't get this particular dog. He looked at me, then at the dog again and thought for a minute and said, "If Tiffany likes this dog, I like him too. Let's keep him, Dad." I was stunned. Kevin chose to keep this dog, and he had done it for me.

I was so touched by my little brother's consideration for me that I said, "Kevin in honor of your lost friend Freckles, let's call this dog Freckles too."

"No, there will never be another Freckles to me," he said. Then, almost as if he could hear my thoughts, Kevin said, "I'm glad we came, Tiffany."

"Huh? What was that you said Kevin?" I asked.

"I said, I'm glad we came to Japan." He seemed to be answering that question I had asked him so many times before. And with that, Kevin had really said it all. He had been thinking about it for awhile now, and he could honestly say that he was glad we had come. Now I had to learn to be glad too. Kevin made me promise that.

I understood then that my brother and I had taken different approaches to settling into our new surroundings. I wore a yukata as a way of trying to "fit in." Kevin saw wearing a yukata as a fun way to discover and explore this place which was new to him too. He ended up "fitting in" much better than me and he had more fun doing it. It was a pretty smart man that said to me, "Tiffany, the way you look at a thing will affect your experience with it."

Then turning toward me, Kevin asked, "Tiffany, please measure me. I want to see how tall I've grown. We've been here in Japan for so long, I must be bigger now."

"You haven't grown that much," I said.

"But I really feel so much taller now," he claimed.

"I guess that's because you have grown, Kevin," I said. "You've grown in ways that can't be measured by a yardstick." And I meant every word.

GLOSSARY

~~~~~~~~~~~~~~~~

Bachan or O-baachan (baa' chan) - grandmother

Bento (ben' tō) - box lunch

Gaijin (guy' jeen) - foreigners

Gomoku (gō mō' kū) - combination, variety

Hashi or O-hashi (ha' shee) - chopsticks

Jichan or O-jiichan (jee' chan) - grandfather

Koinobori (koy nō' bō ree) - fish (usually carp) flags or streamers

Mochi (mō' chee) - rice cake

Mochi-tsuki (mō' chee tzoo kee) - making or pounding of mochi

Musubi (moo' soo bee) - rice ball

Nechan or O-nechan (ne' chan) - older sister

Oishi-katta (oy' shee kat ta) - it was delicious

Shogatsu or O-shogatsu (show ga' tzoo) - the New Year

Soba (sō' ba) - noodles made of buckwheat

Somen (sō' men) - thin, white noodles made of wheat

Tsukemono (tzoo ke' mō nō) - pickles, pickled vegetables

Udon (oo' dōn) - noodles

Wasabi (wa' sa bee) - horseradish

Yukata (yū ka' ta) - lightweight, unlined kimono, used in warm weather

ABOUT THE AUTHOR

Elaine Hosozawa-Nagano, a working wife and mother, now adds author to her list of accomplishments. A graduate of UCLA, Elaine has worked as a writer and producer for an all news radio station in Los Angeles and as Vice President for a national marketing research firm. In spite of family and career demands, Elaine tackled law school. Now, she is taking a little time to retreat to the quiet canyons of Southern California to rest and devote time to her family and her writing. Happily, this "hiatus" has brought us *Chopsticks From America*.

ABOUT THE ILLUSTRATOR

Masayuki Miyata, the pre-eminent artist of the art form called kiri-e, was born in Tokyo in 1926. Miyata's kiri-e encompass a wide range of classcal Japanese literature and include the renowned masterpieces *Oku No Hosomichi*, *Genji Monogatari* and *Manyo Koiuta*. His work has also gained him considerable recognition in international art circles. His *Japanese Pieta* was selected for inclusion in the modern religious art collection of the Vatican Museum. He created *Ganjin Wajo-zo* for the Tosho Daiji Temple in Nara. Six works from his exhibition at Espace Pierre Cardin in Paris were chosen for special entry in the Paris Biennale 100th Anniversary Exhibition at the Grand Palais. In celebration of his artistic career, numerous exhibitions of Miyata's works are being held in Japan and around the world.

ACKNOWLEDGMENTS

This book would not have been possible without the help received from Christopher A. Chen, Kayoko Kawaguchi, Michael and Kay Janis, Yvonne Lau, Jasmin Tuan, Mitchell and Laura Witkowski, George and Vicki Yamate. Thanks also to the LEGO Corporation and McDonald's for their gracious cooperation.

OTHER BOOKS FROM POLYCHROME PUBLISHING

CHAR SIU BAO BOY
ISBN 1-879965-00-3

Written by Sandra S. Yamate and illustrated by Joyce M.W. Jenkin. Charlie is a Chinese American boy who loves to eat his favorite ethnic food, char siu bao (barbecued pork buns) for lunch. His friends have never seen char siu bao before so they think his eating preferences are strange. Charlie succumbs to peer pressure but misses eating his char siu bao. Somehow he has to find a way to balance assimilation with cultural preservation. 32 pages, hardbound (with color illustrations). Recommended by the State of Hawaii Department of Education.

ASHOK BY ANY OTHER NAME
ISBN 1-879965-01-1

Written by Sandra S. Yamate and illustrated by Janice Tohinaka. Ashok is an Indian American boy who wishes he had a more "American" name. In a series of mishaps, he searches for the perfect name for himself. A story for every immigrant or child of immigrants who struggles to be an American. 36 pages, hardbound with paper jacket (with color illustrations). "The book is well-written and would make an excellent addition to a primary school library."--India West.

NENE AND THE HORRIBLE MATH MONSTER
ISBN 1-879965-02-X

Written by Marie Villanueva and illustrated by Ria Unson. Nene, a Filipino American girl confronts the model minority myth, that all Asians excel at mathematics, and in doing so, overcomes her fears. 36 pages, hardbound with paper jacket (with color illustrations). "The book is engaging and delightful reading, not just for this age group [third grade], but for older school children and adults as well."--Special Edition Press.

BLUE JAY IN THE DESERT
ISBN 1-879965-04-6

Written by Marlene Shigekawa and illustrated by Isao Kikuchi. This is the story of a Japanese American boy and his family who are interned during World War II. Young Junior doesn't quite understand what the internment is all about but through his eyes we are able to see how it has affected the adults around him. Fortunately for Junior, he has Grandfather and from Grandfather he receives a special message of hope. This picture book introduces children to the history of the Japanese American internment. 36 pages, hardbound with paper jacket (with color illustrations). Showcased by Teaching Tolerance Magazine.

CHILDREN OF ASIAN AMERICA
ISBN 1-879965-15-1

An anthology of children's stories about the experience of being an Asian American child from ten different Asian ethnic communities. 120 pages, hardbound with paper jacket (with black & white photographs by Gene H. Mayeda).

ONE small GIRL
ISBN 1-879965-05-4

Written by Jennifer L. Chan and illustrated by Wendy K. Lee. Jennifer Lee is one small girl trying to amuse herself in Grandmother's store and Uncle's store next door. That's hard to do when she's not supposed to touch anything. Still, as she goes back and forth between the two stores, Jennifer Lee manages to find a way to double the entertainment for one small girl. A rhythmic and whimsical tale about a small girl's fun fooling big grown-ups. 30 pages, hardbound with paper jacket (with color illustrations). "Kids will delight in the sound effects of shoes clicking on store floors and a small girl's discovery of personal power."--Children's Bookwatch.

ALMOND COOKIES & DRAGON WELL TEA
ISBN 1-879965-03-8

Written by Cynthia Chin-Lee and illustrated by You Shan Tang. Erica, an European American girl, visits the home of Nancy, her Chinese American friend. In her glimpse of Nancy's cultural heritage, she finds much to admire and enjoy. Together, the two girls learn that the more they share, the more each of them has. 36 pages, hardbound with paper jacket (with full color illustrations). "Well crafted. Very stylish for today's America."--The Book Reader.

STELLA: ON THE EDGE OF POPULARITY
ISBN 1-879965-08-9

Written by Lauren Lee. Stella, a Korean American pre-teen, is caught between two cultures. At home, where her brothers get special treatment just because they're boys, Grandmother insists that Stella be a good Korean girl, but at school, Stella is American, aching to be popular and fit in. Can she balance family expectations, cultural values and peer pressure . . . and still be herself? 184 pages, hardbound with paper jacket. "Well-developed characters and a credible plot will hold the interest of readers."--School Library Journal. "An excellent job of detailing the identity conflicts of young Korean American girls."--Asian Week. "A must-read for parents and children."--Korea Central Daily News.

THANKSGIVING AT OBAACHAN'S
ISBN 1-879965-07-0

Written and illustrated by Janet Mitsui Brown. A young Japanese American girl describes her family's Thanksgiving celebration and explains why her Obaachan (Grandmother) makes it so special. Anyone whose family has expanded this American holiday to include reminders of their cultural heritage will appreciate this little girl's Thanksgiving and treasure the memories it evokes. 36 pages, hardbound with paper jacket (with color illustrations). A 1994 Pick of the Lists Selection. "Warm, intergenerational and reminiscent of life with grandmother . . . a family story, beautifully illustrated, lovingly told."--American Bookseller.